W9-AHA-250

Gumdrop 13.50 10/98

The Midnight Game

Strange Matter™
titles in Large-Print Editions:

The Midnight Game

Johnny Ray Barnes, Jr.

Gareth Stevens Publishing
MILWAUKEE

For a free color catalog describing Gareth Stevens' list of high-quality books and
multimedia programs, call 1-800-542-2595 (USA) or 1-800-461-9120 (Canada).
Gareth Stevens Publishing's Fax: (414) 225-0377.
See our catalog, too, on the World Wide Web: http://gsinc.com

Library of Congress Cataloging-in-Publication Data

Barnes, Johnny Ray.
    The midnight game / by Johnny Ray Barnes, Jr.
       p.   cm. -- (Strange matter)
    Summary: Tyler finds a ticket to a midnight football game, a final showdown
between dead rivals who are fighting for the chance to come back to life again.
    ISBN 0-8368-1668-4 (lib. bdg.)
    [1. Supernatural--fiction. 2. Football--Fiction. 3. Horror stories.] I. Title.
II. Series.
PZ7.B26235Mi 1996
[Fic]--dc20   96-19603

This edition first published in 1996 by
Gareth Stevens Publishing
1555 North RiverCenter Drive, Suite 201
Milwaukee, Wisconsin 53212 USA

© 1995 by Front Line Art Publishing. Under license from Montage Publications,
a division of Front Line Art Publishing, San Diego, CA.

Printed in the United States of America

1 2 3 4 5 6 7 8 9 99 98 97 96

TO OUR FAMILIES
&
FRIENDS
(You know who you are)

"C'mon, Tyler," I said to myself. "There's nobody out there. You're the only one left on this football field."

I heard the words come out of my mouth, but I didn't believe them. From my seat at the top row of the bleachers, I could see the whole field. Something definitely moved on the other side; the dark side. I could swear someone was staring at me from those shadows.

Football practice had ended. The sun had almost gone down, and Dad was going to be late picking me up. And I felt sure someone was watching me from across the field.

The wind picked up and I began to wonder, for the millionth time, why I bothered with football at all. I don't like it that much. I play because of Dad. He wants me to learn something about playing on a team.

The only thing I'd learned so far was that something in the dark was watching me and it could come get me at any moment.

I stared until my vision went fuzzy. Was that something moving?

"Hey!" I yelled in my meanest voice. "I see you! I may be a kid but that doesn't mean I'm scared! Actually, I'm pretty brave!"

Then my heart stopped.

A ragged, dusty figure dragged its way from behind the broken wooden bleachers on the opposite side of the field. A hat, dark glasses, and red scarf hid his face. His clothes were grungy with dirt, and covered with patches. A cloud of dust flew off him with every step. The wind picked it up and swirled it, like a dust devil come to life.

He slowly climbed a row or two up the bleachers, then sat with his hands crossed in his lap and his back ramrod straight. He looked right at me.

My heart pounded. Sure, I thought something had been over there, but I didn't really believe it. Not really. It was one thing to imagine somebody out there, but this guy looked real. Were there more like him? If I jumped from the bleachers and ran, could I get away?

Neither of us moved. I stared so intently my eyes ached. The cold wind stung my cheeks and made my eyes water. As I blinked to clear my vision, the dusty man moved.

He dug into his coat pocket. I couldn't see clearly, but it looked as if he pulled something out and laid it down beside him.

Whatever it was, he left it. He climbed down off the bleachers, and the dust cloud around him thickened. I may have been going crazy, but there seemed to be less of him than there was before.

He made his way around the stands, and disappeared into the dark.

I sat and stared for a long time. I looked where the figure had walked away, then back again at where he'd been sitting, and where he had left the . . . thing.

I was terrified, but I was dying to know what it was.

I crept down the bleachers with a lump in my throat and a knot in my stomach. The wind was so strong it nearly blew me off my feet. Trees outside the stadium swayed, as if warning me to go back.

I crossed the field slowly, keeping watch in every direction to make sure nothing was coming after me. The grass seemed to grab at my ankles. Finally, I made it to the other side.

I looked through the bleachers first, afraid something might grab my legs as I started climbing up. Nothing there. I looked, but didn't see anything. Crossing my fingers for good luck, I started up the stands.

As I neared the spot where the man had been sitting, I could see something fluttering in the wind. A spider web. I climbed quickly past it, and found the mysterious object.

A rock. A small rock. I risked my neck crossing the field for a rock? But wait a minute. There was something else under the rock . . . a ticket?

Yes, that's what it was. Worn and faded, but still readable.

"Green Devils vs. Mohawks 12:00 A.M. November 28, 1995."

Midnight? What kind of team plays at midnight?

November 28, 1995 was tomorrow! The ticket looked older than me, but it had tomorrow's date!

Suddenly, a hand grabbed my shoulder.
I screamed.

My shriek could have scared away the dead.
When I finally worked up the nerve to turn
around, I saw the last person in the world I
expected to see.

Dad.

"Tyler - are you okay son? What's wrong?"
he asked.

I felt stupid telling him about what I'd seen.
I didn't want him to think I was a wimp.
"Someone was here, Dad - I don't know where he
went, but he sat right here!"

Dad slowly scanned the field. "Well, I don't
see anyone now. C'mon, let's get home. Your
mom's probably wondering where we are. That
darn battery in the car is acting up again." He
took my helmet and lead the way down the
bleachers.

As we walked off, I looked back into the dark, and thought I caught a glimpse of something in the shadows over by the fence.

"Hey, Dad, I'll race you to the car," I said, and took off running.

Tonight, at least, Dad didn't stand a chance.

During the drive home, I told him the story of the Dust Man (that seemed as good a name as any). Dad was pretty mad at himself for not getting there sooner. One of the reasons we moved to Fairfield was because my parents figured it would be a lot safer than in the city. He told me to stay away from strangers, and wondered aloud if football really was the best thing for me.

That kind of surprised me, because it was Dad who urged me to play for the Timberwolves, Fairfield Junior High's new team. Football isn't really important to me. Dad told me that every kid should try a sport once in his life, just for the challenge and teamwork, if nothing else.

Teamwork wasn't my strong suit. We'd moved to Fairfield, my parents' childhood home, a year earlier and I still hadn't made many friends. It's not that I don't like other kids, I just have a hard time making friends sometimes.

When Fairfield Junior High decided to form

a team, Dad dropped a hundred hints a day until I signed up. He'd played ball when he was my age. I'm probably the only kid in America who doesn't like football but I figured I'd give it a try for Dad's sake.

Even Coach Randall considered me one of the weakest players on the team. On the first day of practice, he'd seen that I didn't know much about football, so he introduced me to his daughter, Libb. She knows everything about the game; plays, strategies, what works and what doesn't, and she's been teaching me. I'd be completely lost on the field without her.

Libb's my best friend in town, maybe my only real friend. I still hadn't meshed well with the other guys on the team. Teamwork hadn't entered the picture yet, since we had yet to play a real game.

When Dad and I got home, Mom began her evening ritual of doctoring the scrapes and scratches I'd received in practice. Most of the time it embarrassed me, but that night I let Mom do her thing. It helped settle my nerves.

Dad held the ticket in his hand, shaking his head.

"Someone's fooling you, son. This ticket's

a fake."

"I didn't make it up. I saw a man leave it there," I told him, wincing as Mom sponged alcohol on my legs. I'm the most germ-free kid in town.

"Well, I'm going to let Coach Randall know suspicious characters are hanging around the field trying to get kids to show up there at midnight. It's funny though. These teams really did play each other once, a long time ago. Your grandfather saw the game."

"You mean the Timberwolves used to be called the Green Devils?"

"No, no. The Green Devils weren't a school team. They were Fairfield's team. They played for the town, not the high school. The players were men who really loved the game. Especially in those days, not everyone was able to go to college or the pros and keep playing."

After dinner, Dad told me to wait while he went upstairs. I could hear him up in the attic, opening the old steamer trunk. In a few minutes he returned and handed me a book.

The title read, "1935 — Our Year." The town's yearbook. It had pictures of parades, fairs, and above all . . . football. Half the book was about football.

"That's your grandfather's book, Tyler."

I studied the pictures eagerly. Everyone looked like they were having a great time. Dad had mentioned things like 'team spirit' and 'town pride' before, but now I could see what he meant.

"The Green Devils lost the championship in 1935," Dad said. "At the same time, bad weather wrecked a lot of homes and destroyed crops. The Great Depression finally reached Fairfield. It wasn't a good time. Lots of folks packed up and left town. Some, like your grandfather, stayed. Things were never the same after that, though."

I was lost in the pictures. Everyone looked like they were having so much fun. Dad had mentioned things like 'team spirit' and 'town pride' before, but now I could see what he meant.

I sneaked the yearbook to bed with me that night. At Dad's "Lights out, Tyler," I grabbed the flashlight from under my bed, pulled the sheet over my head, and flipped open the pages.

There were lots of pictures of the Green Devils' stadium, the field we were playing on now. Only before we started up again, it hadn't been played on for sixty years. It had taken us two weeks and a lot of hard work to get the grass into playing condition. Somehow I didn't think as many people would show up for our games as they did for the Green Devils.

Then I noticed how mean the players looked. Back then football must have been rough. Not as much padding in the uniforms as there is now. They wore leather helmets. Many of the players had teeth missing. They must have wanted to win pretty badly to go through all that.

A lot of the pictures showed the quarterback, Thomas Maul, the meanest looking one of the bunch. Shots of him passing, running, and recovering the ball filled the pages. He even tackled players bigger than himself. I wondered whatever happened to Thomas Maul and all the other players.

A huge yawn came on suddenly, and I lost my place. I blinked to focus my eyes and found myself staring at a new page.

Then, in the background of one of the photographs, in the bleachers, I saw him.

The Dust Man.

3

I didn't sleep much that night, but I didn't mention the Dust Man to Mom and Dad at breakfast either. I needed to tell someone who would believe me, no matter what.

I decided to tell Libb.

School's not my favorite place, but it's okay once I get past math, my first class of the day. Libb and I have math together. We sit in the back of the room so she can make up football plays and show them to me without Mr. Blair noticing.

Libb came up with most of the plays we run at practice. Football is the most important thing in her life. It's funny we became friends at all.

"I call it Play 23," she said, holding up a very detailed drawing of X's and O's. "It's a kickoff play no team can return—a kick sweep to the right."

I happened to be the kicker on our team. I took that position because the kicker doesn't have to play as much as the others. But Libb always drew up plays for me.

"Great play, but I'll never get to use it since there's no other team to play against us. We just practice all the time. Anyway, look at this . . ."

I laid the book on her desk, turned to the page with the Dust Man, and told her my story. She looked at me for a moment, then began drawing on her paper. In a few seconds, she held up the sheet. Another play.

"See this?" she asked. "This is the final play of that Green Devil game. It's an easy run."

"How did you know about it?" I asked.

"Do you think my Dad would coach a football team in this town and not know something about the Green Devils? And everything he knows about football, I know."

"Yeah? Then what do you know about the Dust Man?"

Libb shrugged and then pointed to the team picture.

"I know the records of all of these players," she said.

There were autographs beside the heads in the picture. Grandfather must have known the whole team. Brody Wilson. Jake McGuire. Even Tom Maul. Almost every player had signed the page.

"Your grandfather must have been a popular guy. All the players knew him," Libb said, turning the pages.

"Yeah, I wish I'd known him though. He went down in a plane crash before I was born. Died young, my dad says."

Then it hit me. Maybe some of these people still lived in Fairfield. Maybe they would remember signing this yearbook and would know who the Dust Man was. I couldn't believe I hadn't thought of this before.

All I had to do was get to a phone book. That would be my after school mission—after (sigh) football practice.

Roll call began, and I figured I'd better put the book away for later. As I turned the page over, something caught Libb's eye.

"Oh my gosh, Tyler! Look!" she whispered sharply.

There on one of the last pages I saw the picture of a guy with huge ears and a grin

14

that showed practically every tooth in his mouth. He looked like a goof. I had to laugh, but covered my mouth with my hand so Mr. Blair wouldn't see.

"No, no dummy. Look at the name!" Libb whispered again.

The name under the picture read Herbert Trout.

Herbert Trout is the principal of our school.

Libb and I waited until our first class break. Then we set off to see our principal.

Mr. Trout and I had never crossed paths and I would just as soon have kept it that way.

No one knew how old he was, but I was sure he was the oldest principal around. His face had grown so wrinkled over the years, it looked as if it had been soaking in water forever. Its only bright spot; a glaring white set of teeth. They must have been the healthiest set in town. I wondered if they were false. His ears jutted out from the side of his head like miniature radar dishes. That's how he could hear our thoughts.

Thinking about being in the same room with him, one on one, gave me the willies.

Libb had tried to tell me that Mr. Trout was

just like anyone else. She'd spoken with him before. He could be friendly or mean. It all depended on what kind of day he'd been having.

We arrived at the office, or the Vegetable Room as I called it. The walls were squash yellow and every piece of furniture came in carrot orange or pea green. I figured it was a subliminal way of getting students to eat healthier.

I heard fingers typing at a keyboard, then Mrs Lubfield, the principal's secretary, poked her head up from behind the counter.

"Can I help you, kids?"

"We need to talk to Mr. Trout," said Libb.

She looked at us doubtfully. "He's in the worst mood I've ever seen him. Are you sure you want to see him today?"

"Tell him this is about football," Libb said.

The right thing to say. The secretary hesitated, then pushed the intercom button.

"Mr. Trout?"

"Mrs. Lubfield," a voice replied, so grim it made my blood freeze. "I told you no interruptions before noon."

"I'm sorry, sir. It's Libb Randall and a boy. They say they need to talk to you about football."

A second of silence.

"Hmm. All right, I'll talk to them."

Mrs. Lubfield opened the door, herded us in, then shut it behind us.

The room felt like a cave. Lights out. Shades pulled. Mr. Trout's dark figure sat behind the desk.

"Come in, Libb and friend. Sit down."

The air felt thicker in there than it did outside. Suddenly, this didn't seem like such a great idea.

"Libb," I heard Mr. Trout say, "you wanted to discuss something about football?"

"Actually," she said, "it's Tyler who has the questions."

I gulped.

"Tyler," he said. "You look familiar. What's your last name?"

"Few. Tyler Few." My voice shook.

He didn't sound grumpy. Simply curious.

"Are you Charlie Few's grandson?" he asked.

I nodded, and I think he smiled, but I couldn't tell in the gloom. I took out the yearbook, opened to the page the Dust Man was on, and pointed to him.

"Do you know who this man is?"

Mr. Trout looked at the figure for a few seconds, and then shook his head.

"No. No, I don't," he said. "But this is the strangest thing. Tell me, why'd you pick today of all days to bring this in?" He paused and stared at the wall behind us. "Just last night I dreamed I was driving to a Green Devils game. On the way, two boys jumped out in front of my car and I hit them. Then, this morning, I was driving to work and I could swear I saw my old quarterback on the side of the road yelling for me to come back and play some ball. You know what? I was so flustered, I ran into a tree! And now, you show up with this book! Is someone playing a joke on me?"

I couldn't tell if he was angry or not.

"No, sir," I told him. "This man I pointed out to you, I saw him on the field yesterday, and he left behind this ticket."

I pulled the ticket from my pocket. Mr. Trout took it and examined it, then smiled.

"How's anyone going to play a night game there, let alone a midnight game? There aren't any lights on that field, son. Who'd stay up to see that, anyway?" He stood up, shaking his head. "I think I've been working too hard, and you've been reading too many yearbooks. You two just go on back to class and don't worry about things that cannot be."

Libb and I were still spooked when the final bell rang.

Mr. Trout and my Dad thought this was some kind of a joke. I didn't believe that. Neither did Libb.

"Only one thing to do. I'm showing up at the field at midnight. I have to find out what's going on," I said.

"Tyler, your parents will kill you if you're caught."

I couldn't think of anything else to say, so I shrugged my shoulders and headed for the locker room.

At football practice that afternoon, I had my best day ever. It seemed as if something magical had happened to my foot. One after another, the balls sailed through the goal posts. Even Coach

Randall noticed.

"What's gotten into you, Tyler? The last practice we had, you told me you didn't like this game very much. Now you're kicking like a pro! What gives?"

"Don't know, Coach. Everything just kinda' feels right today," I said.

He smiled. "Hey, everyone!" he yelled. "Since Tyler's kicking so well today, let's run a field goal play."

A field goal play. We had never run a field goal play before. It put me on the spot. The ball would be hiked to Mitch Byrd; he would set the ball up, and I would have to kick it through the uprights before the defense blocked us. Totally my show.

I gulped. I have a bad habit of gulping when I'm nervous.

The defense set up. Warren Dillman, one of the linebackers, looked at me with the meanest eyes I had ever seen.

"I want blood, Few," he said.

Coach Randall blew his whistle once and the defense got set. He blew again and the offense, my team, tensed. The play developed in slow motion for me. It always did when I knew I was going to kick.

I saw the ball float back.

Mitch balanced it in perfect position as I started my run.

All of a sudden, something flashed in my eyes, something bright and twinkling from the other side of the field. I missed the ball completely.

Almost before I knew what happened, Warren Dillman crushed me. Everything went black for a second, then blurry, then wavy, then finally cleared up—sort of. I gazed up at a circle of faces. Some of them were shaking their heads in wonder.

"I've never seen a person's luck change so fast," the coach said.

He helped me up and told me to walk it off. My head felt flat, and Warren smiled because he knew he'd done his job well. I was pretty disgusted with myself. I should have made that kick.

I took the coach's advice and started to jog around a little. I headed in the direction the reflection had come from. After a few steps, Libb ran up beside me.

"I've never seen anyone hit that hard. You've

got to be hurting. And that kick! I've never seen anyone whiff a kick that way before! My dad said the same thing!"

"Ah, give it a rest," I said. "I would have made that kick easy if something hadn't flashed in my eyes."

"If what hadn't flashed in your eyes?"

"I'm not sure. C'mon and help me find it. It should be right up here."

We jogged around the corner at the far side of the field and I stopped. It should be there somewhere, I knew it. I tiptoed through the tall grass, and finally, I saw something reflecting in the sunlight.

A ring.

I picked it up and examined it closely, turning it slowly in my fingers.

It'd been through a lot. The gold was tarnished and it was bent and covered with scratches and dings.

I spit on it to loosen the dirt, then polished it against my jersey. There was an inscription on the inside.

I made out a 'T,' but my vision was still a little blurry. Libb grabbed for it, but I pushed her hand away.

'Thom' . . . I blinked and squinted.
'Thomas' . . .

I caught my breath.

The inscription said Thomas Maul.

The 1935 Green Devil quarterback.

Dad was right on time picking me up after practice and I showed him the ring on the ride home. His jaw dropped when I told him about the inscription.

"Where did you get that?" His eyes shot from the road to the ring and back again. I handed it to him just to keep him from wrecking the car.

I told him the whole story, but when I finished, he looked doubtful.

"Something this small blinded you? This hardly shines at all anymore."

I shook my head. "It blinded me, all right. And guess what? It says Fairfield Champions on it. I thought the Green Devils didn't win a championship."

"They didn't. Terence Fairfield, the grandson of the town's founder, had the rings made up in advance. The team was wearing them the day of the game. After they lost the game, the players took them off. Your grandfather told me they made a pact. Everybody was too ashamed to wear the rings while they were living, but every man vowed to take the rings with them to their graves."

Except Tom Maul didn't, I thought as I slid the ring onto my thumb. "So what should I do with it?" I asked.

"Well, it's definitely a collector's item," Dad said. "Then again, Tom Maul may still have family around Fairfield, in which case they'd get it. The only other ring I know of that still exists belonged to Terence Fairfield. It's in the museum. He had a special ring made for himself with diamonds and an emerald. He always wore it proudly, even after the loss."

I rolled the ring around on my thumb, trying to imagine the gritty quarterback who'd once worn it. Had he lost the ring on that last play? The one Libb had outlined for me? Or had he been so disgusted he'd thrown the ring down and not looked back?

I laid the ring on the yearbook in my lap. "What connection did Grandfather have with the team if he didn't play?" Everyone always made such a big deal out of what a supporter he'd been, but I couldn't imagine being able to top buying rings for the team.

Dad made his I-don't-know face. "Well, that's always been kind of a mystery. I wondered, too, but never found any clippings that said. Grandfather, of course, never talked about it. I think he was pretty disgusted after the loss. I do remember him saying something once about driving everyone home after practice."

"Like a trainer, then?"

Dad shrugged. "I wish now I'd asked him outright, but that was another one of those things I just sort of . . . put off."

I thought about what Dad had said that night as I lay in bed. I rolled the ring around between my fingers, wondering if finding it was a fluke, or a clue to the mysterious events the night before and the ticket I'd found.

My eyelids grew heavy. On the edge of sleep, I drifted back to the football field. I could smell the grass. Taste it as Warren Dillman mashed my face against the turf. I could almost feel the thunder of running feet and the smack of old-fashioned leather football gear.

As I reached over to turn off my lamp, I felt something hop on my bed.

Startled, I looked down at my feet. I saw something scramble across my sheets and over the edge of the bed.

A spider, I thought, but an awfully big one.

I peeked over the side of my bed to confirm my suspicions and then . . .

Something leapt from the floor and grabbed my face.

For a second I was paralyzed, then I took hold of the thing, pulled it off my face, and flung it to the other side of the room.

It landed on my desk.

Everything happened so fast I hadn't even screamed yet. All I did was react. I looked back to the foot of my bed to see what had jumped at me.

There was a hand moving around on my desk. But not a normal, everyday hand. This one was different. No skin. No muscle. Just bone scraping wood.

As I watched, it scuttled around like it was searching for something, then it picked up the ticket to the Green Devils game.

Air left my lungs. I couldn't breathe. My heart had lept into my throat at the sight of something that just couldn't be.

I didn't know what to do, so I decided to wait. When it moved, I would move.

It wiggled the ticket between two of its hideous fingers.

I backed up a bit more, nudging my bed stand.

The ring fell from the head board, rolled off the bed, and hit the floor.

My eyes left the hand for a second to track the ring.

Quick as a cat, the hand jumped from the desk and pounced on my chest. Bones scratched my chin as it tried to shove the ticket down my throat. It was stronger than me, stronger than Warren Dillman even.

I struggled to get it off me but it wouldn't budge. The ticket touched the back of my throat and I gagged, fell off my bed, and landed on the floor.

No way Mom and Dad could have missed that.

They didn't. I heard Dad grumble and get out of bed.

I watched the hand scamper across the floor to find the ring. It scooped up the gold souvenir and let it come to rest on its ring finger.

Then it jumped up to my window, and started scraping at the glass, trying to get out.

Dad came down the hall.

I knew I couldn't explain my way out of this one.

I grabbed my pillow and threw it at the bony claw, knocking it off my window sill and into the waste basket.

Dad opened my door.

"What is it? What's going on?" he said, his hair in a wild state of disarray. Obviously he'd been asleep.

I looked at the window and tried to come up with an excuse.

"Tyler, was there someone at the window?" he asked.

I didn't say a word.

"I'm calling the sheriff," Dad said, and stomped out.

It happened so fast, I didn't have time to stop him.

Now there'd be a million questions that I had no idea how to answer.

The creepy hand rustled through the papers in my waste basket, and slowly crawled out.

Mom tucked me in as Dad talked with Sheriff Drake outside. I could see them on the porch through my window. Sheriff Drake smiled and shook my father's hand, then walked to his patrol car.

I had no idea where the hand was. I didn't know if it had escaped from the house or waited under the bed. It terrified me, but I wasn't about to tell Dad and Officer Drake about an eighty year old hand. They would never believe me anyway. Besides, it had to be gone now. It wanted out, and it would look for any chance to escape, I felt sure.

Dad appeared at my door.

"Well, Sheriff Drake will keep a close eye on the neighborhood tonight, and he alerted some of his fellow officers to look for a prowler. Are you going to be okay?"

"Yeah, I'm all right."

"If this guy shows up again and you see him, come get me. Don't do anything by yourself."

"Dad. He's a prowler. I'm a kid. I'm not going after him by myself. I'll get help, I promise."

"That's my boy," he said, and left my room.

Excuse me, Dad but what I really wanted to say was that the prowler is actually a animated skeletal hand.

The entire episode seemed so bizarre that I felt sure I'd been dreaming.

If I laid down again, closed my eyes and went to sleep, I'd wake up the next morning and everything would be okay. Nothing but a dream.

Trouble was, I couldn't sleep.

I sat up in bed, watchful, my ears straining for the faintest sound.

I noticed the trees outside swaying in the wind, and it reminded me of the football field the day before. More than ever, I regretted playing for the Timberwolves. If I'd never joined the team I'd wouldn't be lying in my bed waiting for something to jump out of the shadows. I'd never have seen the Dust Man. Never have found the ticket.

The ticket.

I looked over to my desk where I'd returned it.

It was gone.

I heard clicking.

Even in the dark, I knew what it was.

The bony fingers scuttled across my room's hardwood floor.

After a second or so, the clicking stopped. I listened hard and reached for my lamp switch.

It jumped on the bed.

Moonlight made the pale bones glow. Again, it held the ticket in its fingers. Tom Maul's ring slid along the third finger. Dad would be upset if we lost the ring, but right now I was willing to give up anything if that hand would just go away.

It crept closer, then dropped the ticket on the bed, as if it were handing it to me.

When I picked the ticket up, the hand sprang to the window sill. It was smarter this time. It crawled to the latch and turned it so slowly I wondered if the pressure on bare bone was painful.

Then it crawled back down and pried at the window, which creaked loudly.

"Shhh," I hissed. "You're making too much

noise. Let me do it."

The hand waited as I got out of bed and went to the window. We both grabbed the bottom. I held my breath, and we lifted. The window opened a few more inches. I sighed with relief as the hand crawled out and landed on the porch.

It crawled to a bright patch of moonlight, then stopped, turning toward me. With its pointing finger, it motioned for me to come along.

9

I waited. The hand waited.

"You're crazy," I whispered. "There's no way I'm going anywhere with you."

The hand moved back and forth. After a few seconds, it stopped. With its finger, it scratched something into the paint on the porch slats. The sound made my skin crawl. Finally, its job complete, the hand stepped back, and I saw the word it had scrawled.

"Grandfather."

"Grandfather?" I asked. "What do you mean?" As if a stupid hand could talk.

Again, the long, bony finger motioned for me to follow. I hesitated, my mind still not made up. I'd told Libb I was going to the midnight game, but no telling what might happen. I wasn't sure I wanted to take the chance.

The finger beckoned again. I wondered what it knew about my grandfather. How it knew that just the word 'grandfather' might be enough to lure me.

All in all, my curiosity was stronger than the fear. I didn't have much choice.

I went to my drawer as quietly as possible and looked for something to wear outside. A black hooded sweatsuit. Perfect! The Ninja Timberwolf. I checked my backpack, still loaded from the time Dad and I went camping a month before. Glad I forgot to unpack it. It had everything I needed; flashlight, mini binoculars, a lighter for campfires, a first aid kit, a folded blanket, a camera and finally, a candy bar and a soda just in case.

Opening the window far enough to get out would be tough. One good, loud creak, and Mom and Dad would come running again. I got it a quarter of the way open and decided that would be enough for me to slide out.

Wrong.

About halfway out, I got stuck. I started to wiggle, trying to pull myself through. Tom Maul's hand danced around with excitement.

That's when Sheriff Drake's patrol car

pulled around the corner.

He was shining a spotlight at each house, looking for prowlers. He would definitely see me. I wiggled with all my might and finally slipped out.

Sheriff Drake came closer. The hand jumped up and down.

I reached back in and pulled the knapsack through carefully. The light reached the edge of my house.

Oh, no! The window!

Closing my eyes, I pulled down the window, hoping it didn't squeak or slam down too hard.

The hand tugged at my hood.

The spotlight beamed across the opposite end of the porch and past my parents' window. Sheriff Drake had arrived. That left only one thing to do.

I jumped.

I landed in the biggest, thickest, sharpest shrub I could have possibly fallen into. I muffled a yelp as Sheriff Drake's spotlight passed over my house and moved down the street.

The hand! Where was the hand?

I felt something moving under me. It inched up my sweatshirt, over my back, and came out right beside my face, crawling like a spider. It hopped out of the shrubs and headed down the sidewalk.

I followed it.

I felt crazy. I'd never sneaked out of the house before. I'd never even been out this late. And I'd never done anything like this behind my parents' backs. I felt like a total bozo. But I still had something to find out.

Grandfather.

Grandfather had gone to every Green Devil game. With all the autographs in his book, I knew how popular and important he'd been to the players. Maybe if the Green Devils really were playing tonight, he'd be there. Maybe I could get the Dust Man to point him out.

Then it hit me.

The Dust Man. Could the Dust Man be my grandfather? Had Grandfather come back to see me? Is that why he gave me the ticket?

I had questions on top of questions, and I was so wrapped in them that I didn't pay any attention to where the hand led me.

Tired and cold, I scarfed down my candy bar for some quick energy. We'd already gone about four miles, and the hand stayed just off the road.

It crept in and out of the shadows, like a little animal. I could barely see it sometimes, but it always made sure I never lost my way.

Then it turned in a new direction, away from the road and through a field.

Then it stopped.

We stood at the edge of the darkest patch of woods I had ever seen.

The hand scurried up to the first trees, motioned me to come along, and crawled into the shadows.

I gulped. Then I summoned all the courage I had, and followed.

10

The hand completely vanished.

I pushed ahead on nothing but faith and sheer willpower.

I used the flashlight for the first few minutes, then switched it off. If someone or something was lurking out there, it would spot me quicker with the light on.

I felt as if the trees were watching me. Tiny things rustled through the pine straw. Sometimes one scuttled over my foot. I tried not to think about what it could be, and kept moving.

I'd never been anywhere else quite so dark. The light from the moon barely cut through the swaying trees. I had no idea where the hand had led me. Couldn't tell north from south or east from west. I gazed toward the moon, hoping to catch sight of something familiar . . .

I tripped.

I must have rolled ten feet down a hill. When I hit bottom, I jumped up. I didn't want to lie on my back in these woods.

I'd dropped my flashlight.

As I felt around for it, I heard something move. Something heavy.

I peered through the dark and saw something even darker.

Looking off to the side, I could see the outline clearly in my peripheral vision.

Someone stood at the top of the hill.

A scream died in my throat. My feet moved faster than I could think.

I ran for the edge of the woods like it was an end zone. I dodged trees and stumps and bumps in the ground like linemen. Sometimes I stumbled, but nothing could stop me.

I could hear it behind me, coming fast.

I knew I had to get out of the woods or be killed.

I saw visions: Coach Randall telling me my luck had changed, Grandfather Few staring at me, daring me.

My heart pounded like a jack hammer as I ripped through the last small stand of trees.

Finally, the open sky greeted me. Moonlight beamed down on the most pleasant sight in the world.

The football field.

Momentum carried me past the crest of the hill. I rolled head over heels all the way to the bottom and came to a stop near the goal posts. It took a moment to regain my senses. It took a few seconds more to remember that whatever had been chasing me probably hadn't given up.

Tall grass rustled at the top of the hill.

A figure emerged, bathed in moonlight.

Libb.

She saw me and half-stumbled, half-fell toward me with a choked cry. Gaining ground behind her were the most grotesque creatures I'd ever seen or smelled.

Zombies, ghosts, or whatever, the things that came out of the woods that night had died a long time ago.

And they were headed straight for us.

12

Libb grabbed me, trying to pull me along with her.

I watched as the creatures came down the hill. It looked like a scene from "Night of the Living Dead". Some of them couldn't keep their balance and started to roll and tumble. A few fell apart, but tried to put themselves back together while still sliding toward us. Every set of eyes locked on Libb and me.

We turned around to run in the other direction, but on the opposite side of the field were more ghouls, groaning and growling and blocking any kind of escape.

They didn't have any skin, at least not the healthy kind. Their bodies looked decayed and ancient. Some, I could see through. Others had wasted away to mere skeletons. Their bones clacked together as they moved.

The smell made me choke as they drew closer.

We were trapped.

Dirt blew up from the field. I grabbed Libb's hand. The dirt swirled so thick I could taste it. Then it swept over us and I couldn't see anything at all. I braced myself, expecting the ghouls to pounce any second. Libb began to cry.

Then I heard another voice. "Why are you here?" it asked.

A thousand reasons raced around in my mind. To this day, I don't know why I said what I did.

"Because I—I have a ticket!"

Instantly, everything went silent. The wind stopped. The deadly groaning ceased. I opened my eyes.

Daylight.

Libb and I stood on the field in full sunlight. Figures still surrounded us, but they were huge men. Football players. They made no move toward us.

The sun blinded me, so I had to squint to see

their faces. They wore helmets, but I still recognized them. Before I could manage to squeak out my surprise, Libb beat me to the punch.

"The Green Devils!"

None of them moved. They merely stood there waiting for something. Libb inched closer, staring at their faces.

"Milo Deck!" She pointed at one of them. "You had the best rushing record for the year. You could dodge rain if you had to! And you're Clinton Booker! Seven interceptions for the first half of the season! Amazing! Tyler, this is it! This is the team! This is the Green Devil team that lost the championship!"

Before I could tell her to shut up, the circle of players began to move. Then I saw another player jogging toward us from the side of the field.

Even from that distance, I could see the look on his face. Intense, like he could eat mud and like it.

The players opened up the circle to let him through. When he reached us, he looked us over carefully.

"Which one of you has the ticket?" he demanded.

My hand shook as I reached into my backpack and pulled out the orange piece of cardboard.

"I do," I said shakily.

I noticed his right hand was wrapped up in a towel. He reached out with his left and grabbed the ticket. Then he stuck one end of the ticket in his mouth and ripped it in two, spitting the halves onto the ground. He looked at me hard, then pointed to the other side of the field.

More players were coming out. Dead ones like before. They wore uniforms, but not in the Green Devil colors. They stood at their end zone waiting.

"That's the team we're going to play," the man said, eyeing them like he hated them all. "But we don't have a field goal kicker. That's why we've got you. You're the only one around these parts."

I looked at him in total disbelief. A team of zombies stood ready at the other end of the field. Ghosts surrounded us, wanting me to play on their team.

I looked at Libb.

She nodded. She wanted me to do it! She was nuts!

"I-I can't play," I stuttered, "I don't have any equipment. I don't have a uniform."

"He has it over there," the player said, pointing to the bleachers.

I turned, and gasped. Over on the sidelines, he appeared.

The Dust Man.

I was starting to panic. Everyone wanted me to do something that scared me.

"I can't do it," I pleaded. "I've never played a game."

Then the hand appeared. The bony little hand that got me into all of this trouble crawled across the field. It was moving in my direction and I thought for a second that it was coming to point me toward something even worse than the predicament I was already in.

I was wrong.

It didn't.

Instead, it ran up to the player, scurried up his leg, and as he lifted his towel-covered arm, attached itself to the nub at the end of his wrist.

The hand had found its home.

Tom Maul.

"You really don't have a choice, Few," he said, looking at the reunion of his hand and wrist. "We're ready to play."

Libb walked me to the sidelines.

"Tell me this is a nightmare," I hissed at her. "Pinch me. Do something!"

"You've got to do this, Tyler," said Libb. "Those are the Mohawks they're playing. The records show that they beat the Mohawks by a field goal in the final play of the game! A field goal, Tyler! That means if history repeats itself, you'll get to kick the winning score! Wouldn't it be fun?"

I caught Libb's arm. "Doesn't it bother you that everyone around us is a ghost? Aren't you concerned that it turned from night into day at twelve o'clock midnight? Say, what are you doing here anyway?"

"You said you were coming, remember? Besides, your ticket said there would be a game tonight, er, today at midnight." Libb lowered her voice as we approached the old, wooden scoreboard where the Dust Man sat. "You didn't think I'd stay home and miss out on something like that, did you?"

"You!" I heard Tom Maul shout out behind us. "Where's your ticket?"

He was speaking to Libb. We had to think fast. It felt like getting caught trying to sneak into a Saturday matinee.

"I don't have one," Libb said, startled and looking scared. "C-Can't I just watch?"

"No. You can't." The other players started to walk toward her.

"Wait!" I shouted, not knowing what to say until it left my mouth. "I need her. She knows all the kicking plays. She's . . . my coach."

Tom Maul looked at me for a moment, and then he said, "I hate coaches, almost as much as I hate the Mohawks. But if it helps you win, well . . . it better help you win. Or else."

Libb and I sighed with relief. We turned back to the Dust Man, who had not moved. He just sat there beside the equipment. I reached for the stuff, never taking my eyes off him.

I couldn't see his eyes for the dark glasses, but I got the feeling he was watching me even though he never turned his gaze away from the field. The same dirty, red scarf covered his mouth.

Fear gripped me, and I couldn't catch my breath. I inhaled deeply, trying to remember the last time I'd been so scared.

Libb must have been terrified too, no matter how brave she acted.

I flicked my gaze toward her, then off into the distance, signaling my getaway plan.

"If you run, they'll catch you," the Dust Man said.

He spoke! I looked at him, my heart pumping so fast I felt the pressure in my throat.

"I want out of here!" I screamed at him.

"The only way out of here is to win this game. If you win, you can go home. If you lose, well, these boys have come a long way to be here. They're not going to be happy if they lose. Especially Tom. This is his game."

He sounded serious. Libb helped me as I put on the equipment, and the jersey and helmet, never taking my eyes off the Dust Man. I looked for anything, anything at all that would show he could be my grandfather.

"My name is Tyler Few," I finally said. "Have you ever heard of that name?"

He turned from the field and, for the first time, he looked at me.

"It's time to play ball, Tyler Few," he said.

A whistle blew, and I turned to the field. Everyone looked at me.

Time for the kickoff.

15

A nightmare. It had to be a nightmare.

I swaggered onto the field like Warren Dillman, hoping no one noticed my knees knocking together. The howling moan of dead things came from the opposing team.

The air grew still. I could almost hear Libb holding her breath. As I got into position behind the kicking tee, I realized the conditions were perfect.

Tom Maul stood near the bench, but I could feel his stare. If I screwed up, he would be there to make sure I never screwed up again.

I looked down the field. The Mohawk receivers looked rotted and moth eaten. It made me sick to look at them. How could they hope to even catch this ball, much less run with it?

Another whistle sounded. I kicked the ball.

The single most perfect kick of my life.

The ball soared high and long.

I saw one of the dead things on the other side of the field leap into the air and snatch it. The Mohawk player bounded across the field faster than anyone I had ever seen.

The Green Devils, my team, ran to cut him off.

I froze. A flash of grinning skull came at me, then musty bones pounced and drove me to the ground. I fell on my back, pinned, and yelled as one after another of the disgusting Mohawk players piled on. I caught a glimpse of their teammate scoring before everything went black.

In the next instant, I was standing on the sidelines and ran out on the field again. I stopped. Something wasn't right here. I looked back to Libb, who sat a few feet from the Dust Man on the bleachers. The scoreboard beside the Dust Man read the second quarter. I trotted back over.

"What happened?" I asked Libb.

"What do you mean?"

"I just kicked off, got tackled, and then all of a sudden I'm headed back onto the field again. What happened in between?"

"After midnight, when the Green Devils

play, time has no meaning," the Dust Man said. "It can be day or night. It can be any year. Or for you, just when you're needed in the game."

I looked at him expectantly, but he wouldn't give me any more answers.

I leaned to Libb and whispered, "Keep asking him questions. Find out who he is."

I remember kicking two more times before Tom Maul made an awesome pass for a touchdown which set up the final play of the game. He played every bit like the football hero the yearbook made him out to be.

Libb had come down out of the stands. She nudged me. "Tyler, this is the last play," she said.

Sure enough, we had a tie score and the clock was ticking. I had to kick the field goal to win the game.

Tom Maul passed me on his way to the bench. "The only way for you to get off this field alive is to make this kick," he said.

Not the pep talk I needed.

Both teams set up.

I glanced at Libb. Tom Maul stood behind her. She looked at me with hopeful eyes.

"I'll make it," I called.

Yeah, I'd better.

Libb's face tensed. She closed her eyes and crossed her fingers.

I took a deep breath as we got into position.

Then the ball was snapped.

I shot forward, praying with everything I had that my kick would be perfect.

My prayers went unanswered.

16

It was, without a doubt, the worst kick of my life.

But it went over anyway.

The field goal was good. We got the points. I had won the game.

No one cheered, except for Libb. She jumped up and down and ran out to the field to hug me. The Mohawk players quietly slumped off the field. So did the Green Devils. No one celebrated.

Then someone picked me up by the back of my jersey.

Tom Maul.

"You did okay tonight, boy," he said. "We'll play again soon."

He dropped me and walked off the field. I looked over at the Dust Man, who remained in the same seat in the bleachers.

"Why are they leaving? Where are they going?" I asked.

"The game's over. They're going back to their resting places until the next game. Some have a great distance to travel. Some are right around the corner."

"Since we won, does that mean it's over? Is this the last game?"

"No," the Dust Man said, coughing slightly as he tried to speak. He reached into his coat and pulled out another ticket. "This is."

He gave me the ticket but I didn't look at it. I looked him straight in the eyes. There was something much more important I needed to know.

"Are you Charles Owen Few?" I finally worked up the courage to ask.

He paused for a moment, then he began to laugh. The Dust Man actually laughed.

Suddenly, the sky crackled and the night returned.

The field and bleachers were empty except for Libb and me.

The Dust Man had vanished.

"Oh, man, this is too weird. C'mon, Libb,

let's roll." I jerked up my backpack and slung it across a shoulder.

Out of the corner of my eye, I saw lights play over the end of the field.

"Uh-oh," Libb said. "Let's get out of here. It's Sheriff Drake."

17

Libb ran and I followed. The woods, once so spooky and dangerous, now felt like welcome cover.

I heard a car door slam, but I had no idea if Sheriff Drake had seen us. I felt like a criminal for running, but I'd have felt worse if he caught us and took us home. No telling what Coach Randall would do, but Mom and Dad would start with grounding me from everything except school, meals, and the bathroom. And things would go downhill from there.

Libb and I ran as fast as we could. Every once in a while, we'd stop and listen, but we never heard anything. No speeding sheriff's cars. No dead guy moans. No lurching zombies coming after us. And then the quiet would get so heavy it would almost crush us and we'd take off running again.

Libb's speed amazed me. She ran faster than anyone on my team, maybe in the entire town. She left the woods minutes before I bounded from the brush.

"Do you think he's still after us?" she asked.

"I don't know," I panted, "but we've got to get back before our folks wake up. It must be almost morning."

"No, it's not," Libb said. "According to my watch, it's only been ten minutes."

"Since what?"

"Since those things started chasing us. Since before we got to the ball field."

I looked at her in shock. Less than ten minutes to play a football game? Not in any dimension I knew about.

"Forget it," I told her. "Let's just go home. We can figure this out tomorrow."

We'd gone a few hundred feet when I noticed that Libb was shivering. It was pretty chilly, cold enough so that I could see my breath.

"Hold up," I told her. "I've got a blanket here somewhere." I had remembered to grab my bag when we left the field. All the equipment had disappeared, but I still wore my cozy warm sweatsuit. I dug into my bag and got a blanket out for Libb, draping it around her shoulders.

The NASA blanket was a light square of foil-like material that Dad called survival gear. It kept rain out and heat in and I figured it was perfect for keeping Libb warm.

As I started to unfold the blanket, I realized the ticket the Dust Man had given me was still crumpled in my fist. I'd forgotten all about it.

I smoothed it out so we could read it. Same orange color, different date, different game.

"This says the Green Devils vs ???," I said. "What the heck does that mean?"

"I guess we'll have to find out."

"You're out of your mind. I'm never going there again no matter how many hands Tom Maul sends after me." I tightened my hood around my face.

"You're just scared because you think you saw your grandfather."

"No, Libb, I'm scared because those people are dead."

The air got colder with every step we took, and my thoughts drifted to my grandfather. Could the Dust Man really be him? If so, why didn't he say anything? Libb's thoughts must have been running along the same lines.

"He might have been scared, your grandfather. Just like you," she said.

"Like me?" Her attitude infuriated me. "Libb Randall, if you had any sense, you'd be scared, too. Dead people shouldn't be running around. They should be . . . somewhere else."

Like the graveyard. Suddenly I knew how to tell whether or not the Green Devils were figments of our imagination. It seemed to me that things didn't crawl out of the ground without disturbing some grass and leaving a trail.

"I know how we can solve this, Libb," I said. "Tomorrow, we're going to the graveyard."

18

"Only a few of the players are buried in Fairfield," Libb whispered to me during math class.

"How do you know?"

"I used Dad's computer to check the newspaper files," she said.

We shut up then because Mr. Blair was glaring at us.

The next six hours of school seemed more like three weeks. Finally, the last bell rang and I met Libb in back of the gym where we'd parked our bikes.

We decided this would be a secret mission, though I don't believe Dad or Mom would have been upset about my visiting Grandfather. But I didn't want to have to explain anything to anyone.

The graveyard was on the opposite side of town from the school. It took Libb and me over an hour to get there. We both knew that it would be dark by the time we got home. But as long as it was light while we were there, we'd be okay. I kept telling myself spooks didn't come out in the daylight.

When we rode our bikes through the cemetery gates and parked them, a strange feeling came over me. It happened every time I came here.

My grandfather rested here.

Dad had brought me here twice before. I never really thought much about the place. Like I said, I never met Grandfather. But as we walked through the graves I had a growing sense of dread.

We reached Grandfather's grave at the top of a hill and everything looked okay. None of the dirt had been disturbed, and the tombstone still stood as it had before. If Grandfather had come back from the dead, he hadn't crawled out this way.

I leaned over the grave and pulled out some of the long weeds that had grown around the headstone.

"He's still here," Libb said.

"The Dust Man must've been Grandfather. I'm sure of it," I said.

I stood up and peered around at the other tombstones.

"Tom Maul's buried around here somewhere," Libb said while she pulled nervously on a loose strand of hair. "Let's look for him."

Libb set out in one direction and I went the other to speed up the search. The grounds seemed to go on forever, hills and flats and little rises. Every time I thought I could start back, I'd find another patch of unexplored plots. Shadows were lengthening. I knew I'd have to turn back soon, but I wanted to finish the search.

I hurried to the top of a hill, hoping to catch sight of Libb and head her way. But when I turned and looked for her, something else caught my eye. All the tombstones—every one of them as far as I could see—stood arrow straight . . . except for one.

I looked for Libb, and saw her on the other side of the grounds. No sweat, I'd check it out myself.

As I drew closer to the unstraightened

marker, I thought about vandals. I'd heard that kids came here in the night to turn over tombstones. That's probably what had happened here. Or maybe the ground became moist and the stone had moved on its own. Whatever the cause, it looked out of place enough to catch my attention.

I stepped to the grave and reached down to brush some moss from the head stone.

There, engraved in granite, was the name . . .

Thomas Maul.

19

I studied it for a long moment. Yes, the stone had moved, but I couldn't tell how it had happened.

Someone had dug a hole where the casket was buried. A man-sized hole. Around it were bits of wood that could be from a coffin . . . but I didn't want to think about that.

I walked closer. If something had crawled out, that meant it was gone, right? Nothing to freak out about. I peeked into the hole, but couldn't see anything. Too dark. I couldn't even see bottom. For a second, I thought I heard breathing, but it was only the blood rushing through my head.

I picked up a pine cone and dropped it into the hole, hoping to hear it hit bottom.

Nothing.

I picked up a rock and tossed it in.

Still nothing.

I leaned over the hole, and spit in it. Still nothing, except that I felt like a jerk for spitting in a grave.

I looked over the hill for Libb, but I couldn't see her. A slight breeze blew, and the leaves from the trees rustled to the ground. Other than that, there was no sound at all. Maybe if . . .

Something grabbed me by the leg!

I hit the ground so hard it knocked the wind out of me. Fingers of steel bound my ankle. I thrashed. Sat bolt upright. Pushed away.

And came face to face with Tom Maul.

The same face I'd seen the night before. He had popped out of his hole and grabbed my leg. Now he began pulling me down to his grave with him.

I kicked and scratched and fought but I couldn't get away. I could hear him grunting out words as he pulled me closer and closer.

" . . . came here to see me . . . well, come see where I live . . ."

No air.

I kept gasping, but I couldn't get any air in my lungs. I flipped on my belly and dug my fingers into the dirt, but I left nothing but a trail of ridges in the soil. I slid halfway in the hole.

Then I got a foothold against his ribs and began to push my way out. He grabbed my pants leg and pulled me down again.

I saw the tombstone starting to tip toward us.

"Too bad you won't make the game tonight, boy," he said. "It's going to be a good one."

Panic made me strong.

I jerked hard and his grip loosened. He still held my shoe. I moved my foot around, trying to get it out of the shoe. Finally, it popped out. The momentum sent Tom Maul crashing back into his coffin. I shot out of the way just as the tombstone smashed down on Tom's head, burying him in the ground. Putrid dust exploded from the grave.

Everything turned quiet.

Finally I could breathe.

I lay still for a moment, sucking in long, deep breaths.

Now I had to find Libb.

I jogged off as fast as I could, staying on the

grass because Tom Maul still had my shoe. He could keep it.

I checked the road for Libb's bike. Still there.

Grandfather's grave. She'd meet me over there, I bet.

Wrong.

I looked around until I saw another tombstone in the distance with the earth dug around it. I ran there as fast as I could. A hole had been dug in the middle of the grave, like someone had come out.

Libb's tablet lay on the ground beside the freshly turned earth.

But there was no sign of her.

It got dark very early that day.

I searched for Libb all over the entire cemetery with no luck. Maybe she was waiting at
the gates where we came in. I jogged there as
fast as I could.

When I got there I found that not only was
Libb nowhere to be seen, but our bikes had
vanished, too.

"I can't believe this. I can't believe it at all!"

I picked up a rock in frustration and threw
as far as I could. Then I picked up another one.
In the minutes that followed, I probably pro-
pelled a bucket full of stones through the air.

When I stopped, I waited a moment to

catch my breath. Anger gone, I realized I had to get help.

I started off down the road as the moon rose, trying to remember the last house I'd passed. It had been a long way away. And now here I was with no bike and only one shoe.

More than once, I thought about giving up. Let Tom Maul have me if he wanted. What good was I, anyway? Libb had depended on me and I'd let her down.

The only thing that drove me, that made me mad, that made me refuse to give up was remembering how deep and hopeless and scary that pit had felt. Maybe Libb was down there. I had to do something to get her back.

The thought pushed me faster. I was practically running when my bare foot came down on something hard and sharp.

A piece of glass . . . yeeooww!!!

My foot bled like crazy, and I knew the chunk had to come out. I gritted my teeth and pulled at it. The sound—yes, there was a disgusting, sucking sound—reminded me to never go out without shoes again. I wanted to cry out from the pain, but I held it in. I took the sock from my other foot and tied it around my cut like a bandage. I held it for a second, putting pressure on it to stop the bleeding. I had to keep going. I had to save Libb.

Then, a few inches in front of me, my other shoe dropped to the ground, covered in dirt.

I looked up.

There stood Tom Maul.

21

I pushed myself away from him and held the chunk of glass up as a weapon. I knew I was dead meat, but Tom Maul just stood there.

"Kicking the ball with that foot could be a problem," he growled. Then he turned and walked down the road away from the cemetery.

He hadn't tried to attack me. He just kept walking, dragging his rotting right foot. It would take his zombie form a long time to get anywhere.

"Where's Libb?" I called out. My mouth had gone into action again before my brain was fully engaged.

He didn't even turn around. "If you want to

find out, I guess you gotta go with me."

He wanted me to follow him. It was like the hand thing all over again except this time Tom Maul had his hand, and I had a hole in my kicking foot. Still, if he'd wanted to kill me, he could've done it by now. I'd follow, but I'd keep my distance.

We made quite a pair, Tom and I. He left a slime trail behind him that glistened in the moonlight. That and the smell were truly disgusting. I hobbled along next to him like a pirate with a peg leg. I kept thinking this had to be a nightmare . . . but it wasn't.

Then I heard something behind me.

I whipped around and saw more of them. More zombies. Dead football players. They moved even slower than Tom.

"They won't hurt you," Tom said as he staggered along. "They haven't the time."

"Where are you going?" I asked.

"The game. The final game."

I stopped dead still. "Hold it," I ordered. My voice echoed off the hills.

Tom Maul kept walking.

"Hey, I've heard of this," I shouted at him. "Something big goes wrong in real life so when you die, you're doomed to repeat it over and over. Is that what's going on? What happens if you win tonight? Is it over? Do you finally rest in peace?"

"Oh, no," Tom Maul rasped. "We get to live. We get to leave the field and return to a town that scorned us. And we get to punish it."

Zombie football players attacking the town? I couldn't let that happen!

I stood stock still, then looked behind me. More of them now, coming out of the moonlight.

I gulped and stumbled closer to Tom again.

"You can't hurt the town," I protested. "There are good people here. The people in town haven't done anything to you!"

"Everyone in this town is weak. They run into bad times, and everyone decides to give up. No guts."

"The team will do anything you say. They play because you want them to. Tell them not to attack Fairfield! Please!"

Tom stopped and looked at me.

"It will take something dead like me to bring this town back to life. I have my reasons." He turned back to his following teammates. "I give them . . . reasons."

"No," I whispered, and looked back at the oncoming zombies.

Then I remembered why I had been at the cemetery in the first place. Grandfather.

"The Dust Man! Where's the Dust Man?" I shouted.

"You'll see him. And your girl friend."

I turned away, and into a light so bright it almost made my eyes pop. When it dimmed, I saw the face of Sheriff Drake.

"Tyler Few! What are you doing here at this time of night?"

"I . . . I . . ."

I looked around, but the zombies were gone. Tom Maul had disappeared, too.

"I . . . I felt like going for a walk?" I said weakly.

22

I sat in my room and watched the clock. I hadn't told anyone a thing, except that I had gone to see my grandfather's grave. Mom and Dad bought it, and didn't yell at me too much.

Libb's parents hadn't called yet. That's not unusual. She stays over at my house for dinner sometimes, and they never call to check on her until around seven o'clock. It was six-forty. I had twenty minutes before they phoned and found out Libb wasn't there. Twenty minutes to live. No way Coach Randall would be as understanding as Dad.

Then I heard a knock at my window. So many scary things had happened lately, I didn't want to look.

Another knock. "Tyler," I heard a familiar voice say.

I felt a rush of relief when I saw Mitch Byrd, the place kick holder on my football team. I went to the window and opened it quietly. If Mom or Dad heard me, I might get into even more trouble.

Mitch smiled, stuck his head inside, and asked politely to come in. I grinned and opened the window wider.

"I hear you're in trouble," Mitch said.

"How did you know that?"

"Sheriff Drake's son Russell listens to his Dad's calls on their police radio at home. He's telling everybody you've been on there two nights in a row now."

"That guy should get a life. But yeah, I've got loads of trouble. Libb's missing."

"What happened?"

I hesitated. Mitch was maybe my only real friend in town after Libb. He was steady and sensible and trusted me without question. He'd never ever flinched in practice, not the tiniest bit, as my foot flew toward the ball only inches from his nose. If I couldn't trust Mitch, then I really was in this alone.

I told him the entire story. From the mysterious man who'd given me the ticket and who I thought looked like my grandfather to the vicious Tom Maul. I told him about the midnight game and about the zombies who played to win the right to come back to life. I showed him the yearbook and told him about the final game of the Green Devils. Finally I showed him the ticket I'd gotten the night before.

"Green Devils vs. Question Mark? What does that mean?" Mitch asked.

"I'm going to have to go to the field again tonight and find out."

"We. We'll go."

"You'll go? Then you believe me?"

"Tyler, I'll let you in on a little secret. Fairfield's full of ghost stories. I've heard most of them, but this is the craziest one anyone's ever told me. What I believe doesn't matter, but no way I'd miss the chance to see what you described . . . if it exists."

"Then you don't believe me."

"I just want to see it for myself. But I'll

help you. The whole team will if you need them," he said.

I couldn't help imagining my Dad with a mile wide grin. *My boy, that's teamwork.* I had to admit, having the whole football team by my side was a comforting thought.

"We may need them. But you and I can check out the field first. I have a feeling that's where we'll find Libb. " I said.

Mitch nodded and slid out the window. Before I followed, I stuffed the ticket into my pocket, but hesitated about taking the yearbook.

"Pssssstttt!"

Mitch startled me. As I whirled, my finger caught the corner of the book. It flipped open to the picture of the Dust Man in the bleachers.

The picture was still old and grainy, but this time it was different.

Beside the Dust Man sat a dark-haired little girl. She looked lonely and cold. She looked scared.

She looked . . . like Libb.

We escaped through my window just as the phone rang. I knew it would be Libb's parents.

Hopefully she wouldn't be missing for long.

I started down my usual path through the woods when Mitch stopped me.

"Where are you going?"

"I go through the woods, and come up behind the field," I said.

Mitch shook his head. "We'll get attacked by zombies in there. It's dark. It's scary. It's zombie country."

Suddeny, we saw the headlights at the same

time we heard the engine. The car swerved straight for us, coming full bore.

I darted off the pavement. Mitch froze like a deer caught in the headlights.

"Mitch!" I yelled. "Move!"

He didn't.

I did the only thing I could do.

I ran back to him, and diving through the air, knocked him to the other side of the road just as the car passed.

I heard the brakes slam on.

A classic, old convertible skidded to a halt in the moonlight. It had to be at least 50 years old. I could barely make out the driver sitting in it.

"Hey, out there!" The person spoke. A young person. "You fellas shouldn't be horsing around in the road. I could've killed you! Hey, come over here, will you?"

We came out of the woods and I heard a chuckle.

"What in the world are you guys wearing?" he asked.

We wore dark sweat suits. Nothing out of the ordinary.

"Why, those are playing clothes. I think you boys are ready for the game. Is that where you're going? To cheer for the Green Devils?"

"Green Devils . . . ?" Mitch began.

"You know about the game?" I asked.

"Fella, everyone within fifty miles knows about the game. I can't wait to get there! Hop in, I'll give you a lift!"

Mitch looked at me. I shrugged. The sooner we got to the game, the sooner we'd find Libb.

When I climbed in beside the driver, I noticed his teeth. They were white and even. And big. Filled his whole . . .

Nah, it couldn't be. Could it?

I introduced Mitch and myself.

"My name is Herbert. Herbert Trout," the young man replied.

I was right. I knew those white teeth could only belong to one man. Herbert Trout, our school principal.

But why was he so young, and on his way to the Green Devils game?

Then I remembered his dream. He'd dreamed that he ran over two boys on the way to a Green Devil game.

We were the two boys! But he hadn't run over us. Instead, he was offering us a ride.

The whole thing was too weird. Trying to

figure it out gave me a headache.

"Thanks for the ride," I said. "We were afraid we'd miss the kickoff."

"Time's a'wasting," he said, jamming the car in gear. "Let's blow low and fly high!"

Mitch's elbow put a dent in my ribs. I'm still not sure whether it was intentional or just thanks to Mr. Trout's bad driving.

"Well, we're almost there," said Mr. Trout. His long hair flopped in his face and he almost ran off the road. "Darn hair. Mom and Dad keep telling me to get it cut but, hey, what do oldsters know?"

It didn't look that long to me. I offered Mr. Trout my ball cap and he thanked me and placed it on his head.

While Mr. Trout drove and 'be-bopped,' as he called it, to odd, old swing music on the radio, I slid the yearbook from my backpack and showed Mitch one of the crowd pictures. There, in a crowd shot of the bleachers, sat Mr. Trout. Same sweater, same tousled hair.

"He might take us to Libb," I whispered quietly enough so Mr. Trout couldn't hear.

"How do you know that?"

"What we're doing right now, it seems like it's supposed to happen. Like it's a clue. Mr. Trout told me the yesterday that he dreamed he'd been on his way to a Green Devils game and he ran over two boys. I bet we're the two boys in his dream!"

"But he didn't run over us," said Mitch, as if that settled everything.

"I know, I know. That's what makes me think we're supposed to be here. Something's going to happen."

Mitch didn't like things being that uncertain, but he settled down, and we watched the road ahead of us. I felt we could trust Mr. Trout to take us to the field. If not, Mitch's idea to jump out would be a good one.

The gravel parking lot beside the old stadium was completely deserted. An uneasy knot formed in my middle. Either we'd missed the game completely or we were way too early. Mr. Trout bailed out of the car as soon as he parked, but Mitch and I stayed put.

Mr. Trout looked in the car window at us like we were crazy.

"Don't you fellas want to see the game?" he asked.

"Sure," I answered. "That's what we came for, but where is it?"

"What are you talking about? The game's right here." With that, he picked up his team pennant and started off.

Mitch and I started after him. We almost caught up, but then he reached the bottom of the hill. He strolled out onto the field and disappeared as if he'd walked through a wall.

Mitch grabbed my arm so hard I felt the bones pop. "HE'S A GHOST," Mitch yelled. "OH MAN, HE'S A GHOST!"

It's the first time I'd ever seen anybody's hair literally stand on end. Mitch scrambled backwards up the hill, lost his balance, and fell on his rump.

"Will you calm down while I check something out?" I asked him. He just tried to catch his breath and stared at the field.

Flipping open the book to the crowd picture, I looked at Mr. Trout. Now he wore my hat.

"I'm going down to the field," I said, closing the book.

"There're ghosts down there. You saw what just happened."

"If I disappear, you run to get help." Then I took off down the hill.

The closer I got, the more the field seemed to vibrate with energy the way heat waves come up off pavement on a hot day. Way in the distance, I could hear a roar. Like ocean waves or heavy traffic. Or a crowd.

I took a deep breath and walked straight on.

Night became day.

A cheering crowd shattered the silence.

I felt pulled apart and reassembled. Not quite here and not quite there.

The stands were filled with people. Players warmed up on the field.

I looked back for Mitch but people were sitting all over the hill. It had to have been the biggest crowd I'd ever seen in my life. I scanned the stands, looking for Libb. She was up there somewhere.

I turned around and saw a player running straight for me. Looking the other way, he didn't see me at all. He leaped in the air to catch a ball and I had to jump out of the way. When he got back up, I looked at his helmet.

It had a Green Devil on it.

"Who are you guys playing tonight?" I asked.

"Are you stupid, kid?" he growled. "We're playing the Razorbacks. This is the championship. Now get off the field."

1935. They'd played that game in 1935.

Then I saw another player running straight toward me. Number 51.

It was Tom Maul.

25

I didn't have time to react.

But he stopped about five feet away, turned, and ran in the other direction. He must have been running a drill.

It felt weird seeing him young and in the flesh instead of dead and rotting. I went over to the sidelines and followed him on his run. When he reached the end of the field, he stopped to rest. Then he looked up suddenly like someone had called his name, and trotted off the field toward the bleachers.

I scrambled after him. If I followed him, maybe I could find out if where Libb was. As I rounded the corner, I stopped short and ducked under the bleachers.

Tom Maul and the Dust Man stood on the edge of darkness, just off the field.

They were talking in low tones.

"Make sure you give them a good show, but throw it away in the last quarter. It'll make the Razorbacks look better in the end," the Dust Man said.

"I'll be leaving town tonight right after the game," Tom said. "You better have the money ready for me."

"It'll be there," the Dust Man said. "You just do your part and you'll have all the money you'll ever need."

It was a payoff! Tom Maul had lost the game on purpose. For money. Nothing but a big fix. This is the guy that wants to come back and "punish the town?" He's no football star. He's a liar and a coward.

I had to tell someone. If I did, maybe the Green Devils could win the game and none of this would ever have happened. But who?

I sprinted around the end of the bleachers, and ran full tilt into the guy who was leading the crowd in cheers. As I bumped him, his Green Devil mask slipped a bit and he dropped his megaphone.

"Hey, fella, going to a fire?" he asked. "Slow down before you hurt someone."

He was the team's mascot. The spirit of the team rested on his shoulders.

The game was ready to start.

He started to pick up his megaphone, but I grabbed it out of his hands, and took a deep breath.

It was now or never.

"Somebody paid Tom Maul to lose this game," I shouted.

I'd aimed the megaphone toward the Mascot. I'd meant for only him to hear. Instead, several people turned my way. A couple of them looked puzzled. One man put his hand to his ear as if asking me to repeat it.

"What?" The Mascot asked. I barely heard him over the noise of the crowd.

"TOM MAUL," I yelled again. "TOM MAUL and this other . . ."

Steely hands clamped around my neck,

jerked me off my feet, and choked off my words. I opened my eyes. Tom Maul's face was inches from mine. He looked murdering mad.

"One more word and it's your last." He ground the words out from between clenched teeth. "We understand each other?"

I nodded mutely. He lowered me to the ground.

"Where's Libb?" I asked. "Where's my friend Libb?"

"Never heard of her." The look he gave me said I was a bug he'd just squashed and was done with.

I watched Tom Maul walk away through an angry, red haze. Team cheers began again, and for an instant I considered giving up on the town. If everyone wanted to follow Tom Maul like sheep, then let them.

I scanned the stands. Libb was up there somewhere. And right now, where the town went, she went. In order to save her, I had to save them all.

I grabbed the Mascot's megaphone again.

"Tom Maul will curse you," I yelled. "Fairfield won't have a football team. People will move away. Believe me. You have to . . ."

This time Maul tackled me outright. I

slammed into the ground. Ate a lot of dirt. Felt my ribs scrape together as my lungs emptied.

The quarterback picked me up like a rag doll and aimed me toward the hillside. He threw a mean forward pass and I was the ball. I hit head first and felt a tingle shoot clear through me.

When I opened my eyes, Maul had vanished. Everything had. The sound, the crowd, the players. All gone.

"Tyler. Hey, Tyler," Mitch yelled.

I stared in amazement. At least half my football teammates came running down the hill toward me.

"Mitch, when I said to get help, I meant the police."

"Mitch didn't come to get us," said Warren Knotts. "We were invited."

He held up a ticket. Just like the one I had. Everyone had a ticket.

I took my ticket out of my pocket and looked at it.

It read Green Devils versus Timberwolves. My team. Our team.

"So when do the other players get here?" Warren asked.

"You'll know, Warren. You'll know."

27

We waited for midnight.

By 11:45 my palms started to sweat.

I knew what would be happening. I told the guys the whole story. They looked really scared. A few wanted to leave but I persuaded them to stay. Safety in numbers, I told them. Teamwork.

Then the moon shone down on the field.

I could feel it starting.

I heard rustling in the trees. Everyone got to their feet, ready to run.

Like light through a smoky glass, the sun broke through.

The first player came out on the far side of the field.

Number 62, Bernie Cook (I had them all memorized by now). He looked awful. I looked at my team. Some stood covering their mouths. Others were frozen in shock, while a few took steps back. I had warned them not to scream. I didn't know what the dead things would do if we screamed.

One by one, the Green Devils filtered in. Some stumbled to the field, others crawled. But once they touched the green grass, they stood up and breathed like they could taste the air.

Then a Green Devil came out of nowhere and ran through my team, knocking down a couple of the guys. He joined his teammates on the other side of the field.

"Tom Maul," I said.

At the other end of the field, I suddenly saw someone different. No, two people. They walked toward us. By the limp, I knew one had to be the Dust Man. As they drew closed I could finally tell who was walking with him.

Libb.

He had her by the back of the neck. They stopped and he motioned me to come over.

Dead players came over the hill behind us, and we had nowhere to go but on the field. We stayed in a circle, making sure none of them rushed us. Inching toward the edge of the field, I heard the raspy voice of Libb's captor.

"Come here," he said insistently.

I shook my head.

Then he shot out his hand and I heard the sickening popping of bones as his arm stretched ten feet and grabbed me by the leg. I kicked and fought, but he pulled me right up to him and looked down at me.

"Let me give you the score," he said. "Tom Maul's guilty spirit won't let any of us rest. We've waited sixty years to be able to end this. You and your team are our chance."

I gulped. "What do you mean?"

"We either want to live again, or to rest peacefully. The only way to do that is by playing a real live team and winning. Your Timberwolves are the first real team to play in Fairfield since Tom Maul disgraced us."

You helped disgrace the team, I wanted to say. But I didn't dare. What if this man really was my grandfather? And if I made him mad, what might happen to Libb?

The dead players edged closer. We had to do something soon.

"One touchdown, winner take all," the Dust Man rasped. "Besides, you don't have anything to lose. If you try to run, they'll kill you. If you lose, we get our lives back and we still kill you. If you win, we rest in peace."

I looked at Libb.

She nodded. She wanted me to agree.

I looked at the team.

Trapped.

The only way off this field alive would be to win.

"Okay," I said.

The temperature dropped a few degrees as we waited to start. Mitch winked confidently, but I saw fear in his eyes.

Warren Dillman's hands were shaking. My knees felt like Jello on a hot day.

My team waited in a line for me on the field. I knew that some of them wanted to scream, or to cry, and mostly to run, but they didn't. We would play our first game that night, and we'd play it as a team.

The dead players were shaking too, but not from fear. Many were falling apart. Legs and hands dropped off of some as we got ready for the coin toss. I figured that was a good sign.

Maybe we could win if the other team fell to pieces.

Something grabbed me and hoisted me into the air.

In a split second, I looked into the bulging, yellow eyes of Tom Maul. He still had teeth and a face so moist that it steamed in the cold.

"I've waited sixty years to win the big game. Sixty years to make it up to my team, and I will. They'll live again, and my slate will be clean. That's the deal I've made. It's just too bad there's no glory in beating the likes of you."

He threw me back to the ground.

"Flip the coin," he demanded.

The Dust Man pulled a coin from his pocket.

"Wait!" I said to him, "where's the referee?"

"We don't have a referee. Heads or tails?" he asked.

"Then let Libb flip it!" I said.

"I don't want to flip it!" she yelled.

"Just flip the coin!" Tom shouted.

"Libb, flip the coin!" I said.

Libb took the coin and flipped it into the air.

"Heads," I said.

It hit the ground with a soft thud.

Tails.

Tom Maul backed away, and then turned and walked slowly to his team. His face looked so mangled I couldn't tell if he was smiling or not.

I looked at the Dust Man.

"This is your fault. He took your money and lost the game for you. If he wins tonight, it's on your head! Can you live with that?"

The Dust Man grimaced. "I don't want to live at all anymore. I hope you win so I can rest in peace."

Libb's fingers dug into my arm.

"Play 23. Hold tight to the right side," she whispered. "And watch number 80."

I trotted out to the huddle. Our first huddle in a real game. A game we *had* to win.

"What did Libb say?" Warren asked. I could swear he had a new patch of white hair on his head.

"Play 23. That's a kick to sweep to the right. I read in the yearbook that old Bruce Deal is the best kick returner they have to that side. He's number 80, the one with no skin. His legs look pretty weak to me, so let's see what we can do."

We lined up, ready to kick.

At best, I have trouble with ball control, but

now my toes felt numb and the cut on my foot burned like fire.

I looked at Libb. She had her fingers crossed.

The Dust Man stood still in the wind, with the play whistle inches away from his mouth, not making a move.

Finally, I looked straight down the field at the ghastly, moaning things from the grave. In a few seconds we might all switch places.

I thought about Grandfather's picture, Dad's words of encouragement, and how I really wished I had practiced more so I could play better.

The whistle blew.

I ran up to the ball and kicked it so hard, I fell on my back.

A high, beautiful kick.

It nearly touched a cloud, then came spinning down to land in the dead Bruce Deal's hands.

I thought being dead would have made their legs too brittle to run fast.

Wrong.

He took off like a streak.

My team went after him, but when they met the Green Devil offense it was like running into a blender. We were knocked in the air, thrown to the ground, and slammed to the side so hard, I knew this would be the only play many of us would be able to make.

I got to my feet. Only Warren and I stood in the way of a Green Devil touchdown. Warren would get to him first.

"His legs, Warren," I screamed. "Go for his legs!"

Warren dived, grabbing dead Bruce's legs. They came right off his body. The rest of Bruce fell to the ground and the ball popped out of his hands.

I quickly scooped it up, and saw an army of zombies coming my way.

"Run!" Libb cried. "Run or you're dead!"

30

No time to think. I ran. Tried to avoid anything that would kill me. The Timberwolves were scattered about the field, getting up slowly, dazed.

Bony hands grabbed at my shirt but I ran so fast it ripped their hands off. I had at least four fists gripping my jersey. None of them were attached to arms.

A Green Devil dove for my feet but I hopped out of the way. He splintered into pieces when he hit the sideline bench.

I sprinted for all I was worth. I don't know if

it came from fear or from the excitement of getting away from all the things chasing me.

Libb was screaming for me to keep going. The Dust Man just stood there like a statue.

At last, only one stood in my path.

Tom Maul.

The only one between me and my end zone.

I zigged left, he zigged left.

I zagged right, he zagged right.

He was as quick and smooth as my shadow.

Seemed to know every move before I made it.

So I lowered my head and ran right at him.

Five yards away from the end zone I dove into the air. Tom reached up to grab me, but I went right through him, and rolled into the Timberwolf end zone.

My first touchdown. But what a nasty one!

The daylight faded into a gathering darkness. The field was bathed in the light from a glowing moon.

Bits and pieces of Tom's middle hung all over me. I looked back at him to see what I had done. He had a hole clean through his center. I suddenly realized he was screaming.

He fell to the ground and started over to me.

I didn't have the strength to move when he grabbed me by the jersey and pulled me right into his face.

"How . . . how about the best two out of three?" he asked.

"Sorry, Tom," I said, "I don't make deals."

He collapsed in a heap and didn't move anymore. I sucked in my breath and got up, never taking my eyes off of him.

Then the worms came up, hundreds of them. They began to feast on Tom Maul. Dirt poured through him like a river, and the grass sprouted up to finish the job. The Earth couldn't wait to get hold of him.

31

The rest of the dead began to gather their bodies and return to their homes, where this time, they would stay.

The Timberwolves seemed to be coming around okay.

I walked over to Libb.

She stood beside the Dust Man. He had fallen to the ground.

"He was laughing," Libb said. "He clapped when you made the touchdown."

"Who are you?" I asked him for the final time.

"Me? I'm Terence Fairfield. My grandfather created this town, and preserving it is the most important thing to my family. I wanted it to stay like it is to this day, small and quiet. A big football team would have brought a lot of people here. We didn't need a lot of people. We're a small town, and I had to keep it that way."

"Tell me," I demanded, "what did my grandfather have to do with this? What do you know about Charles Owen Few?"

For a moment, I thought he was going to answer. But he waited too long. The worms came again, then the Earth ate him, too.

No answers.

Libb nudged me. "Look," she said. "Up there."

I turned to see the outline of the Green Devil mascot, standing at the top of the hill with the moon lighting him from behind.

Slowly, he lifted his mask. I could feel his eyes on me.

Instantly I knew.

My grandfather had been the mascot.

He'd been the team's biggest fan because he embodied the spirit of that team.

He raised a hand and, staring straight toward us, gave me a thumbs-up. Then he backed over the hill and disappeared.

My team had broken the spell. Now Grandfather and the whole Green Devil team could rest in peace.

As the field consumed the rest of the dead, and my team picked themselves up, one by one, Libb let me in on a secret.

"When my Dad wanted to start a team in Fairfield, he couldn't decide if it should be football or tennis. Maybe I should tell him that a one on one sport would be better."

"No," I said. "I sort of like this game."

And now
an exciting preview
of the next

STRANGE MATTER™

#3 Driven to Death

by Marty M. Engle

The tops of the masts rose high in the glass case. The sails, made of real cloth and tied with real string, hung low, crisscrossed with plastic rigging.

The captain's wheel could actually turn, moving the rudder with it.

The removable cannons pointed out from windows cut in the rounded plastic sides.

I remembered painting each piece of trim and gluing each crate to the deck.

I peered through one of the windows and saw the tiny skeleton chained to a wall in the brig, even tinier plastic rats glued all around him.

"That took forever to get right," I said to myself as I stepped back from the old masterpiece gathering dust in my garage.

My name is Darren Donaldson. I am thirteen years old and I love building models. I have been building models for three years now and have become very good at it. Dad says I have a real talent.

The garage held quite a collection. A beautiful eighteen wheeler truck with a trailer and working lights (it gave me nothing but trouble and took two weeks to put together). A nuclear submarine nearly three feet long. A bunch of ships from Star Wars, and my crowning achievment; the crown jewel in my collection and a source of admiration from all my peers.

A pirate ship.

The moonlight, shining through the dust of the tiny windows in the garage door, would light up the sails and take your breath away.

At Fairfield Junior High, it is widely regarded as the most beautiful model every assembled. Painted in every detail; dry-brushed wooden planks to make it look old; small rips in the sails; spray painted smoke stains around every opened cannon window.

I read about a dozen books on pirates

before I started, to be sure of every detail.

Dad put it in a glass case for me on the day I moved it to the garage from my room.

That became the saddest day of my life for two reasons.

One, it meant I had to start looking for other places to store my models or get rid of some old ones. Something I couldn't even think about and. . .

Two, it was the first time my older brother David didn't help me finish a model.

David always helped me put the finishing touches on my models and never took any credit for it. We always had a great time, painting and sanding and detailing. He would be the first to brag about my attention to detail and painting expertiece.

But this time he barely acknowledged my existence. He seemed mopy and sad and wanted to be left alone. We hardly did anything together anymore.

Except on Thursday movie night. Dad would make us both go to the video store with him and the whole family would watch whatever we rented. I love watching movies almost as much as building models, especially scary ones.

The one thing David and I agree on is the type of movies we rent. What else? Horror movies!

Mom hates it when we rent horror movies, but Dad lets us get away with it, if it's not too scary.

Anyway, I walked over to the car and waited. The garage lights were off. The moonlight streamed in through the windows, striking the sails of the ship and filling them with light. I could have watched it for hours.

Then David turned the lights on.

"Shotgun," he muttered.

His bad mood practically oozed out.

"No way! I was here way before you. I get the front!" Rules are rules, after all.

"Shotgun," David said again as he jumped in the driver's side and slid over, locking the front door.

I puffed up, ready to clobber him when I heard Dad coming down the stairs to the garage. I am not very tall, but I'm stocky and I love a good fight, especially with David.

"NO SCARY MOVIES!" Mom yelled

down the stairs as Dad popped into sight, keys in hand.

"Ready to go, guys?"

Dad loves movie night almost as much as I do.

"You bet, Dad." I slapped David's window as I hopped in the back seat. I wouldn't let the grump king of the universe ruin my movie night.

The grump king grumbled and sulked in his seat as the car started.

"C'mon David. Give it up. I am not letting you hang out at McDonald's parking lot all hours of the night. Friends or no friends. It won't kill you to spend a little time with your family."

"YEAH! Tell him, Dad!"

David let his seat fall back and hit me in the head. His smile filled the rear view mirror.

"Get off, moron!" I shoved the seat back up and flipped the back of his ear.

"Enough, Darren," Dad said. "I promised your mother we would get back quick. David, are you going to be a spoil sport all night?"

"No," David sighed. He didn't fool either

of us. He would be the grump king until we got there, then he would snap out of it. Same thing happened every Thursday.

Until now.

About the Authors

Marty M. Engle and **Johnny Ray Barnes Jr.**, graduates of the Art Institute of Atlanta, are the creators, writers, designers and illustrators of the **Strange Matter**™ series and the **Strange Matter**™ **World Wide Web page.**

Their interests and expertise range from state of the art 3-D computer graphics and interactive multi-media, to books and scripts (television and motion picture).

Marty lives in La Jolla, California with his wife Jana and twin terror pets, Polly and Oreo.

Johnny Ray lives in Tierrasanta, California and spends every free moment with his fiancée, Meredith.